For Mo, who always supported
my sense of adventure – C.D.

And for Miranda and Remi.

All rights reserved. Published by Arthur A. Levine Books, an imprint of Scholastic Inc., *Publishers since 1920*.
SCHOLASTIC and the LANTERN LOGO are trademarks and/or registered trademarks of Scholastic Inc.

Library of Congress Cataloging-in-Publication Data
D'Amico, Carmela.
Ella sets sail / by Carmela and Steven D'Amico. – 1st ed.   p. cm.
Summary: When Ella the elephant goes to the carnival and loses her lucky hat in a storm,
she learns a valuable lesson about the real meaning of luck.
ISBN-10: 0-439-83155-5   ISBN-13: 978-0-439-83155-0
[1. Storms–Fiction. 2. Carnivals–Fiction. 3. Luck–Fiction.
4. Elephants–Fiction. 5. Animals–Fiction.] I. D'Amico, Steven. II. Title.
PZ7.D1837El 2008   [E] – dc22   2007013833

10 9 8 7 6 5 4 3 2   09 10 11 12
First edition, June 2008   Printed in Singapore
Book design by Steven D'Amico and David Saylor
The text was set in 20-point Aged.

ella

sets sail

by carmela & steven d'amico

ARTHUR A. LEVINE BOOKS

An Imprint of Scholastic Inc.

The Elephant Islands Carnival had come to Little Village.

Ella was meeting her friends there.
"Have fun," her mother called.
"I will!" Ella waved. She'd looked forward
to the carnival all summer.

But halfway there, a strong gust of wind knocked her hat off her head.

Ella sighed. "I can't believe it. What could be more unlucky?"

By the time she found her friends, the rain had almost stopped. "What should we do first?" Ella asked.

"I must win one of those parrots!" said Belinda, stamping her foot.

"It's no use," Frankie warned. "The game is fixed."

"It never hurts to try," said Ella.

"That's right!" Belinda agreed. "Let me borrow a coin, Ella. Please? Just one?"

"What happened to your money?" asked Ella.

"I already spent it," Belinda said.

Reluctantly, Ella handed Belinda a coin.

"I know!" shouted Belinda. "You don't want your coin to go to waste, right? So let me borrow your lucky hat, too."

"Well…I'm not sure."

"Pretty please?" Belinda begged.

"Oh, all right," Ella said.

While Belinda waited in line, Frankie and Ella and Tiki played around in the House of Mirrors.

"I'm so big!" Ella gasped.

"Look how long my legs are!" Tiki giggled.

Outside, the Parrot Man began shutting down his booth for the day.

"Sorry, folks! The parrots aren't so fond of stormy weather," he explained.

Belinda decided to cheer herself up by spending the coin Ella had lent her...

...on one last Ferris wheel ride.
"Where's Belinda?" Tiki asked.
"Up there!" Frankie pointed.
"And there goes my hat!" Ella cried.

"I have to get it!" she exclaimed, and took off running through the crowd.

Ella looked all around for her hat.

Finally, she found it.

Where is Mr. Pelican? she wondered. *If he knew how important this was, I know he'd let me borrow a boat.*

Ella had to row far and fast to catch up with her hat.

"I've got it!" she said.

The rain was falling harder. The waves were growing taller.
Ella tried to row back to shore, but the boat drifted farther and
farther away.

I'll use my lucky hat as a sail, she thought. *It's never failed me before!*

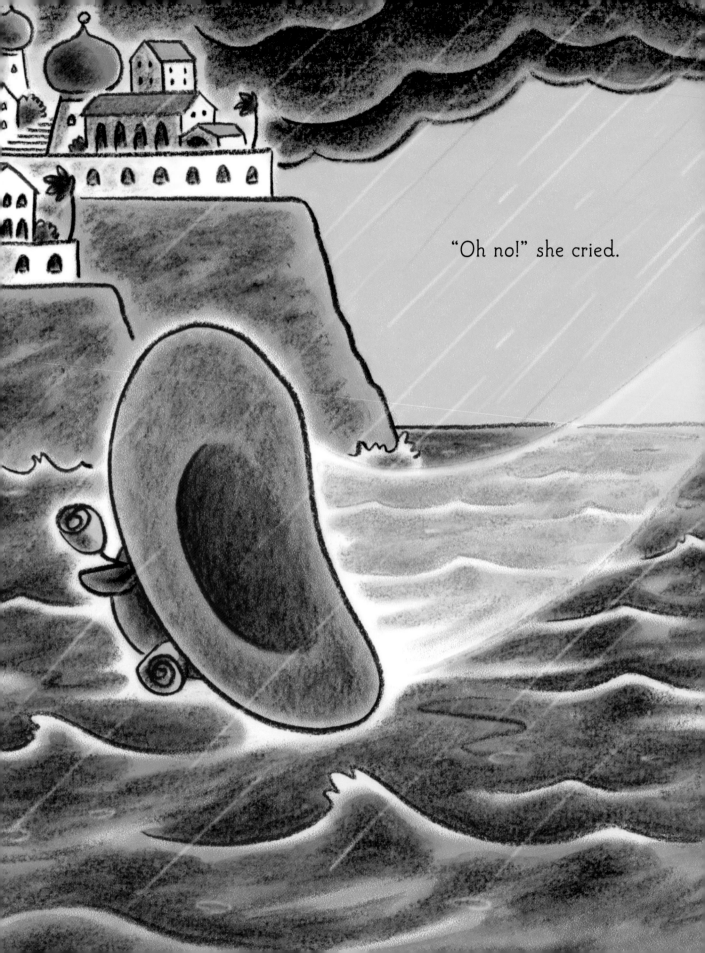

"Oh no!" she cried.

Had she ever had a day in her life that was more unlucky than this one?

At last, the boat washed ashore on an
island she'd never visited before.

Ella wandered into town.
"Would you like to come in out of this
terrible weather?" a kind voice called.

"Thank you," Ella said, and burst into tears.
Then she told them about her very bad luck,
and how her hat had blown away after all.

"Well, you're safe now," Mrs. Spindle smiled, "and just in time for lunch."

The children asked lots of questions about Little Village and her mother's bakery.

"You've never had pineapple pie?" Ella asked.

"Never," the children said.

Soon, Mr. Spindle arrived.

He said to his wife, "I have something for you. A fancy thing it is, too! Got caught up in our fishing net during the final haul."

Ella was thrilled to see her hat, but she didn't want to ruin Mr. Spindle's gift.

The storm had passed, so she had to hurry home.

"Good-bye," Ella said. "You've made me feel so welcome."

"Hold on there," Mrs. Spindle said. "Aren't you forgetting something? What's the chance of another red hat turning up in a fisherman's net?"

"Oh, thank you!" Ella said.

"Good-bye!" shouted the children. "Come back soon!"
"I will!" Ella waved as she started home.

Ella arrived to find Mr. Pelican busy fixing a boat.
"You must have bananas between your ears, taking
a boat out during a storm like that," he called.
"I'm sorry," Ella said.

"Well," Mr. Pelican grumbled. "You're just lucky nothing happened to my boat."

"Ella, where have you been? We've been looking all over for you," said her mother.

"Sorry about your hat," said Belinda. "It was an accident, honest."

"I'm glad you're okay," said Frankie.

"Yeah," Tiki agreed.

Walking back to the bakery, Ella told them everything that had happened.

"Goodness, Ella!" her mother said. "That was some adventure! But promise me you'll never take a boat out in stormy weather again."

"Don't worry," she said. "I promise. I won't."

Ella asked, "Could we bake a
pineapple pie?"
"Certainly," said her mother.
"May I ask what for?"
"It's a surprise," Ella answered.

The next morning Ella headed back to the docks with a freshly baked pineapple pie to share with her new friends.

"You really gave me a scare yesterday," Mr. Pelican
scolded. "You're lucky I don't tell your mother. You're
lucky you're alive. You're lucky—"

"You're absolutely right," Ella said, smiling...

"*I am* lucky."